P9-BJE-083

Swimming in the Sand

BY MARCIA LEONARD

PICTURES BY JOHN WALLNER

Silver Press

For James Robert Leonard, Dunewood's newest beach boy.
— M.L.

For Marcia with affection.
— J.W.

Produced by Small Packages, Inc.
Text copyright © 1989 Small Packages, Inc.

Illustrations copyright © 1989 Small Packages, Inc.
and John Wallner.

All rights reserved. No part of this book may be used
or reproduced in any manner whatsoever without written
permission from the publisher.

Originally published by Silver Press, a division of
Silver Burdett Press, Inc.
Simon & Schuster, Inc.

Printed in the United States of America.

ISBN 0-8136-3404-0

10   9   8   7   6   5   4

Hippo was hot! The midday sun beat down on her house. The air was muggy and still.

"If I sit here much longer, I'll melt!" she said. "I need to go somewhere breezy, someplace I can cool off!"

Now where do you think Hippo decided to go?

Did she go sit in the attic
and sulk?

Did she go soak her toes
in a hot tub?

Did she take a bus to
the beach?

Or did she move to a tent
in the desert?

Hippo packed her beach bag and picnic basket and took a bus to the beach. She changed into her bathing suit in the ladies' dressing room. Then she walked along the shore, looking for a place to sit.

She found the perfect spot near the water,
opened her umbrella, spread out her blanket,
unpacked her bag, and sat down. *Whew!*

The sound of the waves was soothing. The breeze from the water was cooling. But Hippo was still hot.

So what do you think she did next?

Did she go swimming
in the sand?

Did she wrap herself up
in the blanket and cry?

Did she smear her face with
peanut butter?

Or did she go splash
in the waves?

Hippo jumped and splashed in the waves.
At last she felt cool and comfortable!
Then she put on her mask, snorkel, and flippers
and dove underwater to look for pretty stones.

When she came up for air, she saw a
friend nearby. "Hi, Elephant," she called,
"that inner tube looks like fun!"
"Would you like to try it?" he asked. "We could trade."

So that's just what they did.
They stayed in the water so long, their skin turned
wrinkly. "Maybe we should get out now," said Hippo.
"Okay," said Elephant. "What would you like
to do next?"

And what do you think Hippo replied?

Did she say, "Let's build
a sand castle"?

Did she say, "Why don't we
vacuum the beach?"

Did she say, "Let's put on our
Halloween costumes"?

Or did she say, "Why don't we
make a snowman?"

"Let's build a sand castle," said Hippo. She got out her pail and shovel, and they made a huge castle — with towers, a moat, and a drawbridge.

Soon after that Elephant had to go home.
But Hippo did not want to leave. The sun was still
high, and she knew her house still would be hot.

"Time for a little something to eat," she said.
She shook the sand from her beach blanket
and sat down very carefully.

Then what do you think she did next?

Did she call for a waitress
and ask for a menu?

Did she open her picnic
basket and have a snack?

Did she gnaw on some
sunglasses sprinkled
with sand?

Or did she plant an apple
and wait for it to grow
into a pie?

Inside the picnic basket was a Hippo-sized snack:
a thermos of lemonade, an apple, an orange, a bag of
carrot sticks, three sandwiches, four cookies, and five
mints. Hippo finished it all. Then she took a nap.

When she woke up, the sun was going down and the air was lovely and cool. By now her house would be cool, too. It was time to go home.

But Hippo lingered just a little longer to watch the sunset paint the evening sky.